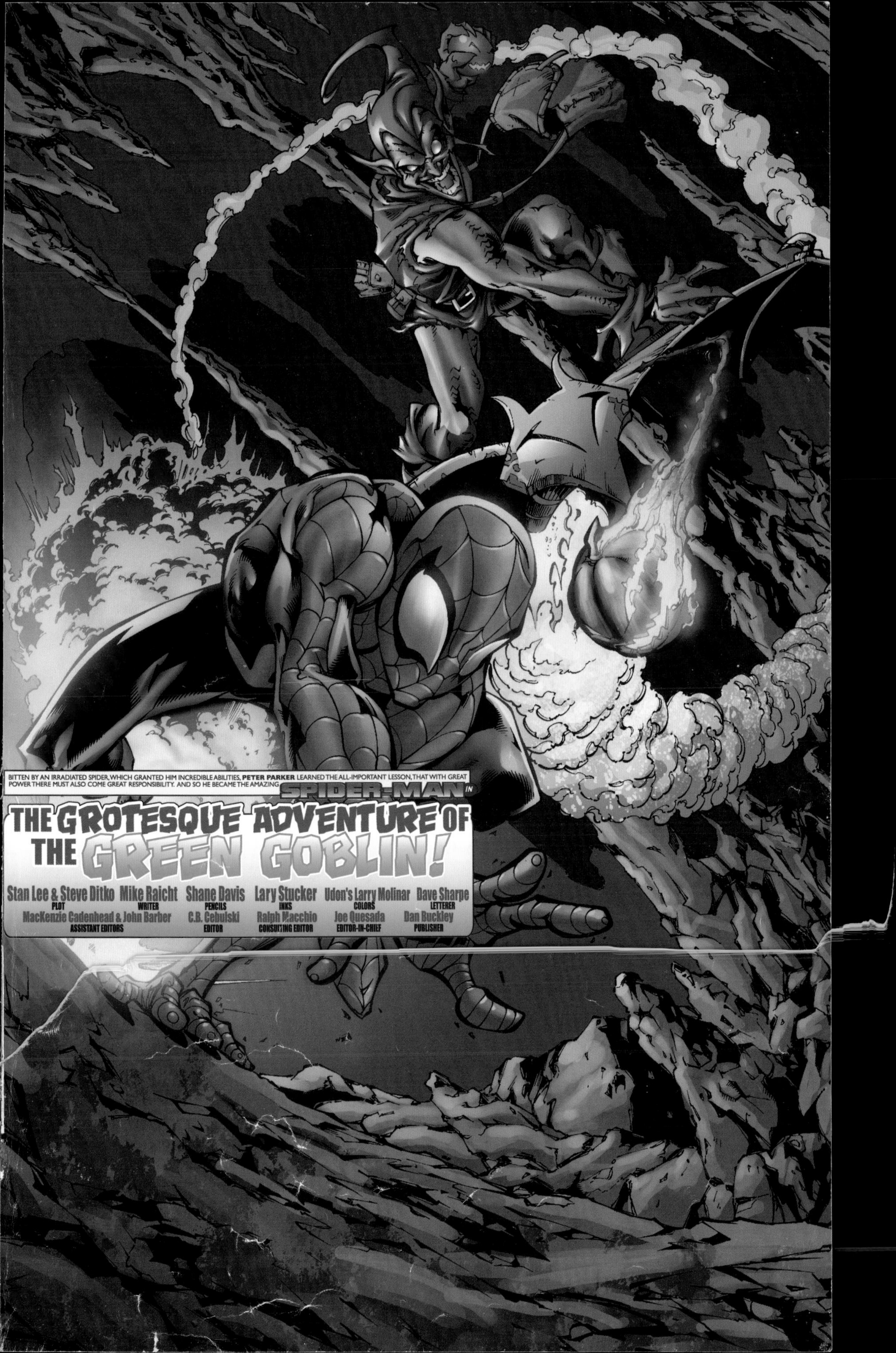
BITTEN BY AN IRRADIATED SPIDER, WHICH GRANTED HIM INCREDIBLE ABILITIES, PETER PARKER LEARNED THE ALL-IMPORTANT LESSON, THAT WITH GREAT POWER THERE MUST ALSO COME GREAT RESPONSIBILITY. AND SO HE BECAME THE AMAZING SPIDER-MAN IN
THE GROTESQUE ADVENTURE OF THE GREEN GOBLIN!
Stan Lee & Steve Ditko PLOT
Mike Raicht WRITER
Shane Davis PENCILS
Lary Stucker INKS
Udon's Larry Molinar COLORS
Dave Sharpe LETTERER
MacKenzie Cadenhead & John Barber ASSISTANT EDITORS
C.B. Cebulski EDITOR
Ralph Macchio CONSULTING EDITOR
Joe Quesada EDITOR-IN-CHIEF
Dan Buckley PUBLISHER

VISIT US AT

www.abdopub.com

Spotlight, a division of ABDO Publishing Company Inc., is the school and library distributor of the Marvel Entertainment books.

Library bound edition © 2006

Library of Congress Cataloging-in-Publication Data

The Grotesque Adventure of the Green Goblin!

ISBN 1-59961-020-5 (Reinforced Library Bound Edition)

All Spotlight books are reinforced library binding
and manufactured in the United States of America

A secret laboratory...
It's working.
I've finally gotten the formula right! I feel the strength coursing through me.

And now with my inventions and newfound super-strength, the world will know--

--that the *Green Goblin* has arrived!

A motel room nearby...
Why are we here? We don't even know who this Green Goblin guy is...
Chill out, Montana.
The guy is paying us to be here. We're in a penthouse suite!
You should be happy we're getting cash for nothin'.

RRIIPPP!
NEW!
Well, if he doesn't get here soon I'm gonna do this to him, Dan.
Ox, come on man...what am I doing here with you guys?

I'm sorry to keep you waiting, Enforcers. I know your time is expensive but I have plenty of money so I'm sure you won't mind.
I've got a plan--

Hold up! We've followed the leader before and it didn't work out.
This is my gang now and we're not taking orders from a freak like you.
We'll take your money but we do the job *our* way.

WHAM!
OOFFF

I understand your concerns. But I'm paying for this, so you'll listen to me.
I think once you hear who I'm after you'll be more than happy to go along with my plan.
How would you like revenge on the man who humiliated you?
How would you like to take down *Spider-Man?*
The offices of Cosmos Productions...
Yes, I know. This guy gave me a blank check to fill out if I would help him film this movie.
Who? You wouldn't believe me if I told you.
But he's claiming he can get me the real Spider-Man.
I know it sounds crazy but imagine if we pull this off.
We'd be the only studio with a *real* super hero movie.
Cosmos Productions and B.J. Cosmos will be household names!

Midtown High School, the day before Spring Break...
Your aunt must be really proud of you, Peter. No one gets the grades you do.
I just study hard, Liz. You're just as smart as I am.
We could study together if you want to.
Suuure. That sounds like a lot of fun.
Cut it out, Flash. Just because Peter and I care about our futures and not just sports doesn't mean you have to pick on him.
Hey, easy. I was just...
See you, Peter. Have a good break.
Maybe we could *all* study together?
Hey, guys! Check this out.

The news says they don't know who this guy is but they think he's dangerous!
Every time someone gets close to him he flies away yelling about Spider-Man.
I've got to go...to you know... to get home and study. See ya.
Study? Spring Break just started. Parker's such a geek.
Hey, Greenie!
Wait up!
I heard you wanted to talk to me.
You could have just taken an ad out in the paper...
...that's what other guys have done, at least.
Spider-Man! Finally!

I've been circling for hours.
Yeah. I heard. You're scaring people.
I've been sent to set up a meeting between you and Cosmos Productions.
I'm sorry... what now?
B.J. Cosmos is in the city and he wants to make you a movie star.
Why didn't he find me himself?
How would he have gotten ahold of you?
True. But--
No buts. He's waiting for you in the penthouse suite at the Ritz.
It's a great opportunity. I'm in the movie, too!
Don't think about it. Just do it!

The Ritz...
Hello?
Spider-Man!
Come in! Come in!
So, here's the deal. We'll give you six figures to star in this movie.
Six figures?
We can't go any higher.
Sounds great!
The movie will be you taking on the Green Goblin...who I'm assuming you've met, and a group of stuntmen who will be playing the Enforcers.
Are you in?
CONTRACT
No interviews or press. I don't want anyone to find out who I am.
I could care less who you are, buddy.
CONTRACT
X Your Friendly Neighborhood Spider-Man
My only concern is the millions we're going to make together.

You won't regret this, Spider-Man. We are going to be richer than you could ever imagine! I'll see you in California.
See you there, B.J.!
The Daily Bugle...
So, you're on Spring Break, huh, Peter?
What are you going to do?
JAMESON
Well, actually, Betty, I think I'm going...
Parker! Just the man I wanted to see.
I've got a scoop for you.
Uh--hey, Mr. Jameson. You scared me.
Actually, sir, I've got a trip planned to California and--
That's perfect! I've got a lead that says Spider-Man is going to try to parlay his crime activities into a movie career.
And since you'll already be there, I won't have to pay for room and board. Now get going!
Sure thing, sir.
Be careful out there, Peter. Hollywood is crazier than New York.

Later...
But Aunt May, it's a chance for me to make some real money taking photos on the set. Mr. Jameson even said he'd pay for the expenses.
Oh, I don't know, Peter. It seems like quite a trip for someone your age.
Aunt May, I would never let you down. You have to trust me. It could get us way ahead.
Will this make you happy, Peter? Do you think some time away doing this will cheer you up?
Yeah, I do.
You're always so serious...okay, you can go.
Thanks, Aunt May!
You're welcome. Just please, be careful.

Los Angeles, Ca.
Okay, Spidey, here's the deal. We're starting with a lot of the stunt stuff first to get it out of the way. When I yell "action" just do your thing.
All right, people, let's get the show on the road.
When do you want to jump him, G.G.?
Just give the word.
Patience, Dan. Though I'm happy you've decided to go along with my plan, it will require waiting for the right time to strike.
Hey, B.J.! Shouldn't we get some practice first?
These stunt guys are a little nervous about working with a real super hero like Spider-Man.
You know what, you're right. What do you think, Spidey?
Makes sense, I guess. I don't want to hurt anyone.
I don't really know how to fake fight.
I've got to say that you guys look great!
I fought the Enforcers once and you look just like them.

Although to be honest, the real Dan was a lot uglier.
Haha... uh...ha.
B.J. wants to start with the big fight scene so let's practice that one.
Um...I haven't really read the whole thing yet.
I kind of assumed that we'd start at the begin--

Whoa! Hold up! Let me read what we're doing first.

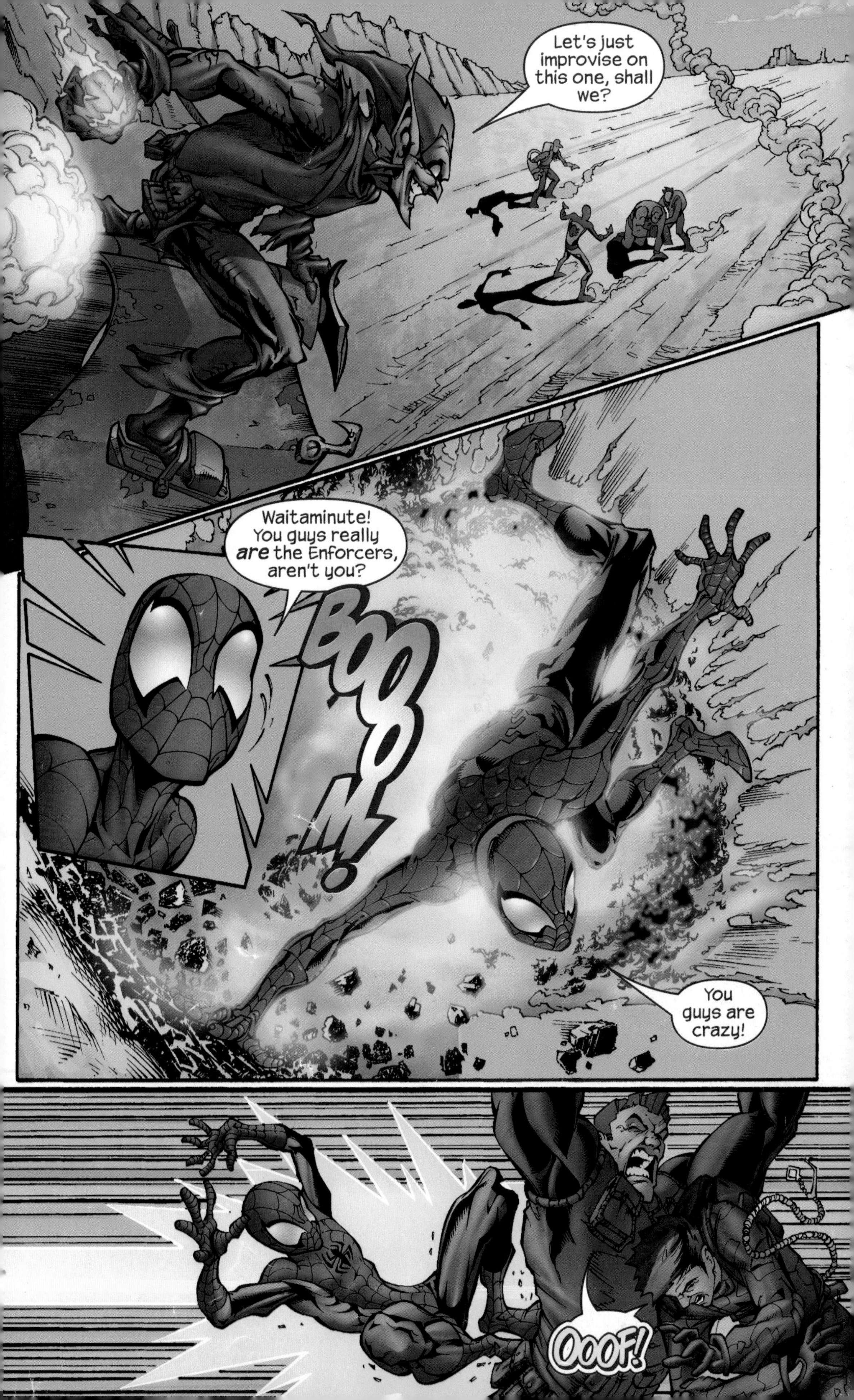
Let's just improvise on this one, shall we?
Waitaminute! You guys really *are* the Enforcers, aren't you?
BOOOM!
You guys are crazy!
OOOF!

A lasso? This is the best you can do?
It worked, didn't it?
Ox, you get the first shot.
One squashed spider, coming up!
WHAM!

Spider-sense is still going nuts.
There are just too many of them--coming at me from all sides...
Owwwww... I can't concentrate on--
Just hold that pose a second longer.

Uhhh!
Noooooo! I can't see!
CRASSSHHH!
Where did he go?
He's gone!
I know...
The only place with any cover out here is that mine shaft.

Got the wind (huh) knocked (huh) out of me.
Maybe they won't come in here, Parker. You never know.

It's pretty dark in here, Dan.
How are we gonna see 'im without our night vision in there? I don't think it's a good idea to go in blind. Maybe he's got some freaky spider-vision or something.

Is that better?
You don't have to go in, Ox. Watch the doorway and make sure he doesn't escape.

Fine. Then you two spread out and find him...
Hey guys, did you see these huge footprints in here?

They're gigan--aaaahhh!

Dan?

Forget him! Just find Spider-Man!
I've got a bad feeling about this.
Hey, Ox! Goblin! Help!
He's over here!
I'm coming, Montana! Hold on!
Wow! You really *are* dumber than you look!
Now on to find your fearless leader.
Oh don't worry, Spider-Man!
I've found *you!*

BLOOOOOOOOM!!
Look out!

HAHAHAHAHAH!
That Goblin guy's crazy!
Ya think?

We've gotta get out of here.
What now?

RUN!
Oh, man.

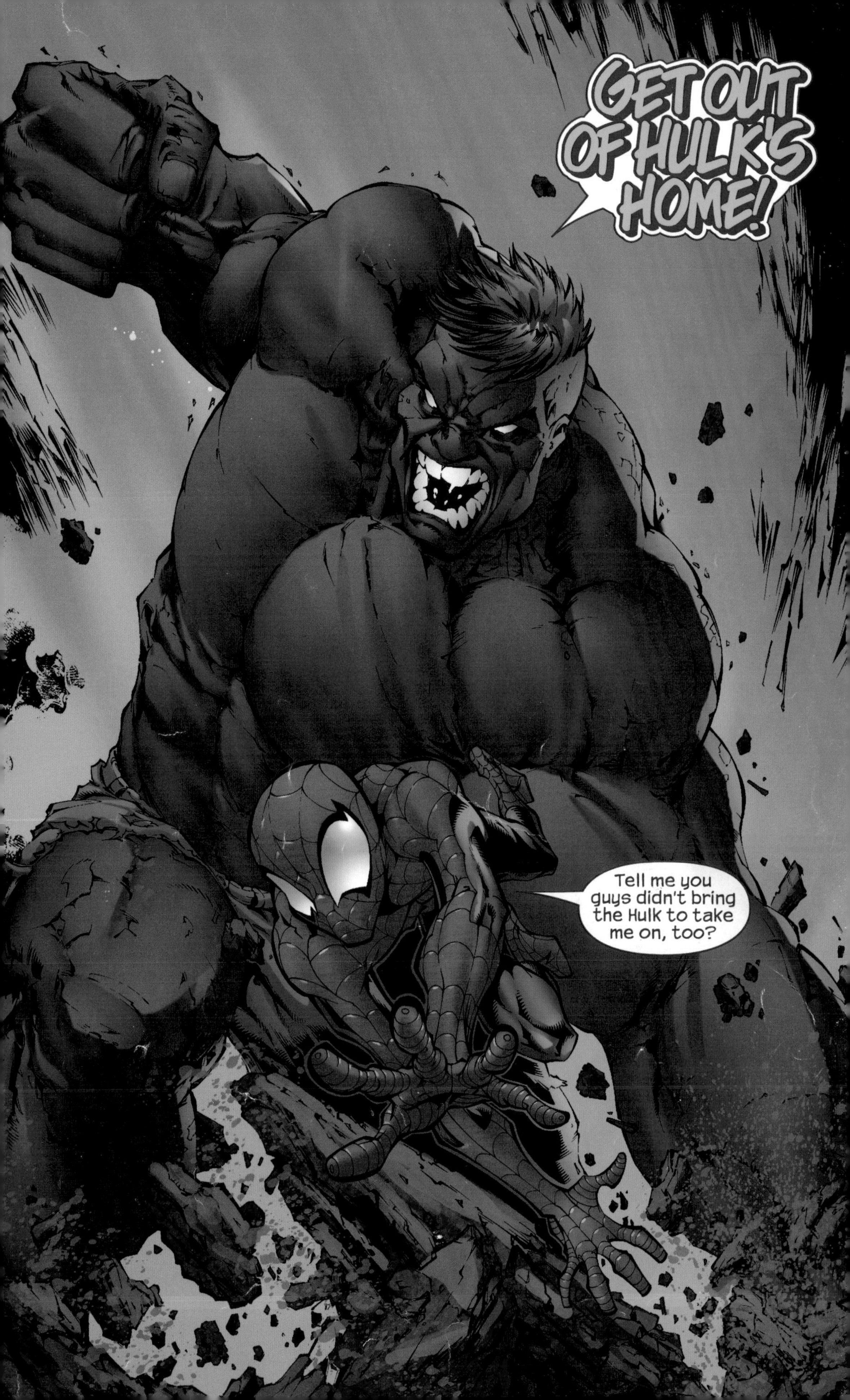
GET OUT OF HULK'S HOME!
Tell me you guys didn't bring the Hulk to take me on, too?

Montana, we have to get out of here!
uhhhh...
Ox, Dan is near the front of the cave! Grab him and get out!
The Hulk's going nuts!
Arrrrhh! Get out of Hulk's home!
Believe me, I want to!
Oh, Spider-Man, it will be so much fun to watch the Hulk pummel you--
Wha--? No, you idiot!
NO!
I'm out of here!

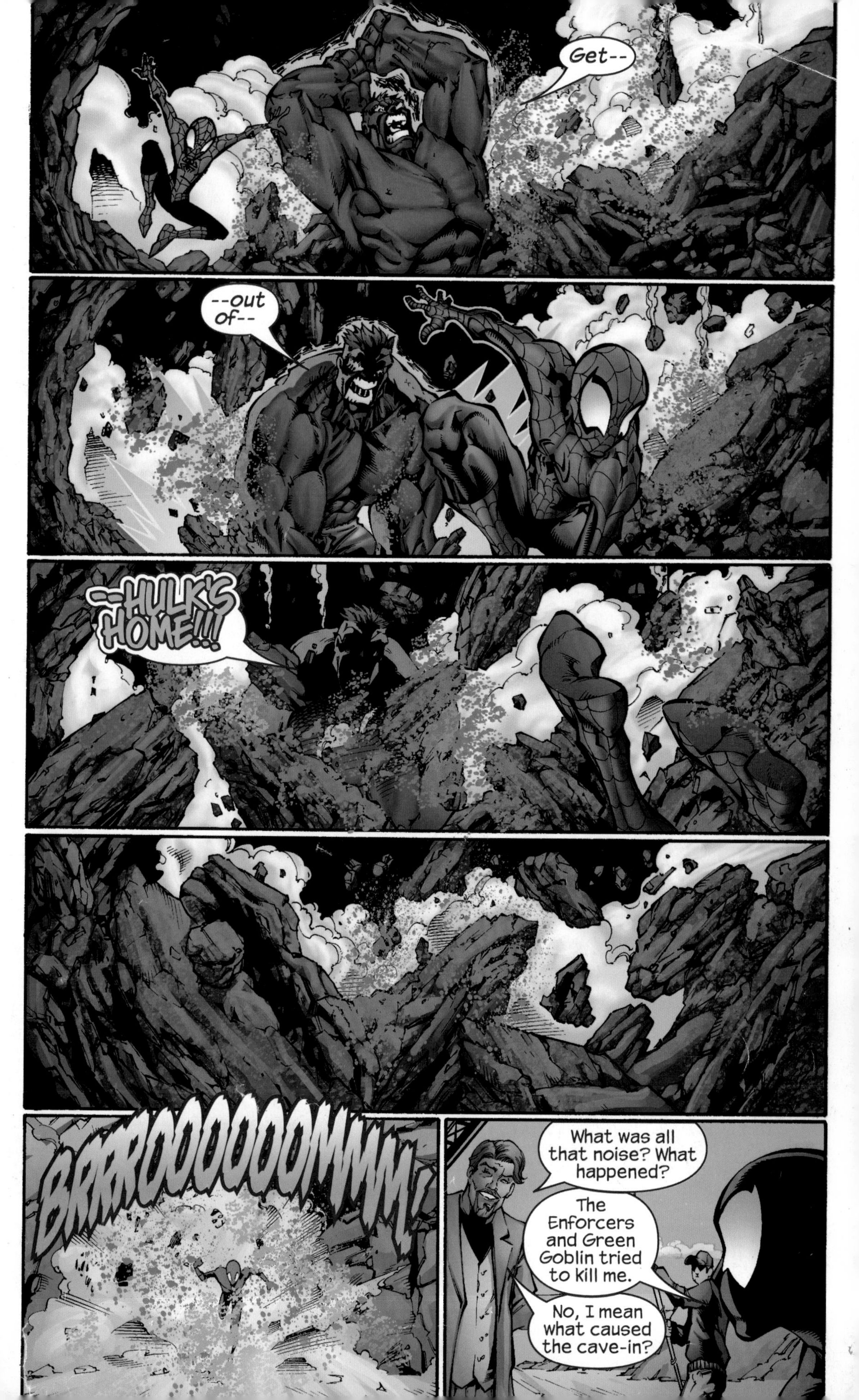
Get--
--out of--
--HULK'S HOME!!!
BRRROOOOOOMMMM
What was all that noise? What happened?
The Enforcers and Green Goblin tried to kill me.
No, I mean what caused the cave-in?

The Hulk is in there and--
The Hulk? Do you know how much money a Hulk movie could fetch me?
A Hulk movie?
But what about the Spider-Man movie? I signed a contract.
A contract that is void if we don't finish the shoot. Which we won't be able to without the rest of the cast.
Read the fine print. And always bring a lawyer, kid.
For your expenses and a bus ride home.
All right, gang, let's get some digging equipment and try to get some Hulk footage.
You've got to be kidding...
A mile away at the other end of the mine shaft...
This is not the last you'll see of me, Spider-Man!
HAHAHAHHAH!
"No, Mr. Jameson. I didn't get any pictures."
Later...
COFFEE
What?! I heard the Hulk was there! And some new costumed freak called the Green Goblin!
My bus is here--I've got to go.
Maybe they're all in cahoots together! Spider-Man...the Hulk...the Green Goblin!
If only I had some pictures of them working together, Parker!
...Parker?
Parker?
HULK
End.